GRAPHIC SCIENCE

THE EARTH-SHAKING FACTS ABOUT

EARTHQUAKES

WITH MAX AXIOM

SUPER SCIENTIST

Katherine Krohn

illustrated by Tod Smith and Al Milgrom

www.raintreepublishers.co.uk
Visit our website to find out
more information about
Raintree books.

To order:
☎ Phone +44 (0) 1865 888066
📄 Fax +44 (0) 1865 314091
💻 Visit www.raintreepublishers.co.uk

Raintree is an imprint of Capstone Global Library Limited, a company incorporated in England and
Wales having its registered office at 7 Pilgrim Street, London EC4V 6LB
Registered company number: 6695882

"Raintree" is a registered trademark of Pearson Education Limited, under licence to Capstone Global
Library Limited

Text © Capstone Press 2008
First published by Capstone Press in 2008
First published in hardback in the United Kingdom by Capstone Global Library in 2010
The moral rights of the proprietor have been asserted.

ISBN 978 1 4062 1460 4 (hardback)
14 13 12 11 10

British Library Cataloguing in Publication Data
Krohn, Katherine E.
Earthquakes. -- (Graphic science)
551.2'2-dc22
A full catalogue record for this book is available from the British Library.

Art Director and Designer: Bob Lentz
Cover Artist: Tod Smith
Colourist: Krista Ward
UK Editor: Diyan Leake
UK Production: Alison Parsons
Originated by Capstone Global Library
Printed and bound in China by South China Printing Company Limited

Acknowledgements
The publisher would like to thank the following for permission to reproduce copyright material:
Shutterstock p. 24 (map, Sean Gladwell)

CONTENTS

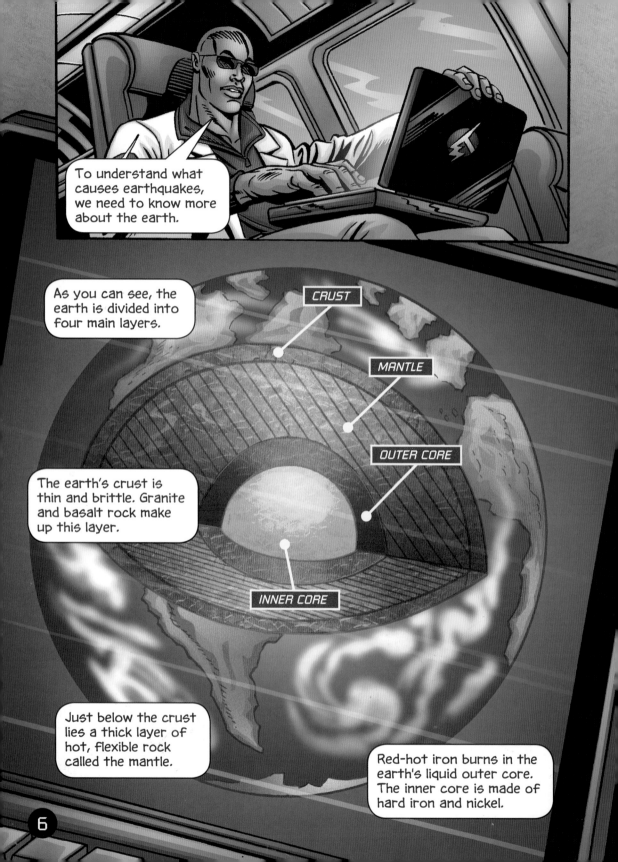

To understand what causes earthquakes, we need to know more about the earth.

As you can see, the earth is divided into four main layers.

CRUST

MANTLE

OUTER CORE

INNER CORE

The earth's crust is thin and brittle. Granite and basalt rock make up this layer.

Just below the crust lies a thick layer of hot, flexible rock called the mantle.

Red-hot iron burns in the earth's liquid outer core. The inner core is made of hard iron and nickel.

We live on the earth's crust.

The crust is divided like a jigsaw puzzle into giant pieces called tectonic plates.

But unlike puzzle pieces, tectonic plates don't always fit together.

TECTONIC PLATES

ASTHENOSPHERE

The earth's seven major plates ride on top of the upper layer of the mantle called the asthenosphere.

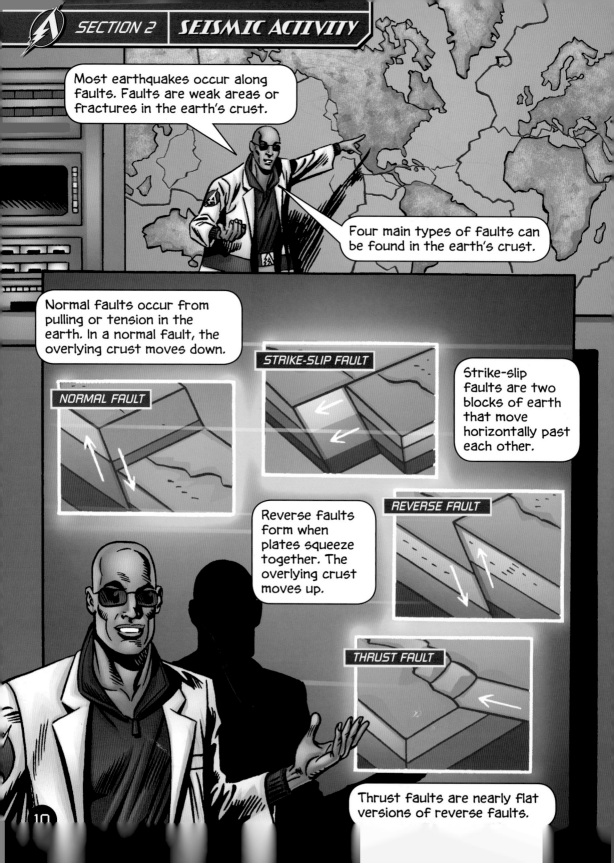

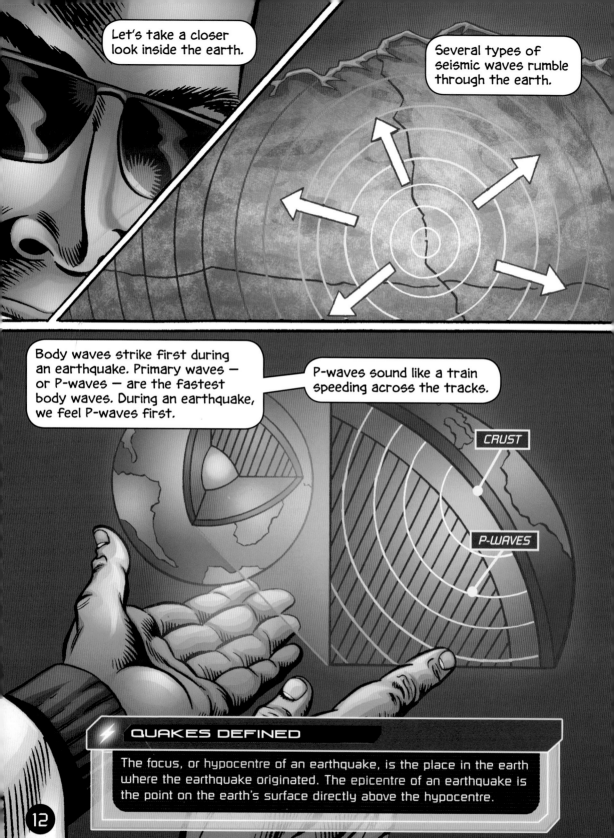

Powerful quakes of all levels have been shaking the earth for billions of years. It's only during the last few hundred years that scientists have been recording data about these monster quakes.

The New Madrid Fault zone in Missouri runs along the Mississippi River in the US. On 7 February 1812, a magnitude 8.0 earthquake occurred there.

What is that horrible rumbling sound?

It's an earthquake!

SHOCKS

Smaller earthquakes that happen before a large quake are called foreshocks. The highest magnitude earthquake is called the mainshock. An aftershock is a smaller earthquake that follows the mainshock.

The 1812 earthquakes destroyed nearly half the town of New Madrid, the quake's epicentre. Fortunately, few people lived in the newly settled territory. Only one person died in the disaster.

Another earthquake!

Get outside! The house could collapse on us!

For several days after this devastating quake, the area experienced aftershocks. Aftershocks can occur for days or even years following a large quake.

Earthquakes occur underwater too. On 27 March 1964, a massive earthquake jolted the calm waters of Prince William Sound, off the coast of Alaska in the US. This earthquake had a magnitude of 9.2.

The 1964 Prince William Sound Quake was the largest earthquake ever recorded in North America.

Within 24 hours, several large aftershocks hit the coast of Alaska. Many buildings were destroyed by these aftershocks.

SMITH & MILGROM

When earthquakes happen underwater, they can generate huge waves called tsunamis. The 1964 earthquake created a tsunami that struck the upper west coast of the United States and Canada.

A tsunami isn't just one wave, but a series of waves that travel in all directions across the water. When this wall of water crashes into a shoreline, it can be deadly.

Nearly 90 percent of the earth's earthquakes and volcanoes occur in one main region of the earth.

This horseshoe-shaped region along the Pacific Ocean is called the Ring of Fire.

The area got its name because of the many earthquakes and volcanic eruptions that happen here.

Scientists here in Taiwan and around the world have been researching the Ring of Fire region for years.

They are trying to better predict where and when earthquakes will strike. I'm eager to learn more about their findings.

Unfortunately, people can't always prepare for earthquakes. Old buildings in ancient cities are easy targets.

In 2003, an earthquake with a magnitude of 6.6 rocked the city of Bam, Iran. More than 40,000 people were killed in the quake.

MORE ABOUT EARTHQUAKES

About 500,000 earthquakes are detected by seismologists in the world each year. Of these earthquakes, only about 100,000 of those can be felt. Only about 100 earthquakes each year cause damage.

Scientists have learned that the crustal plate of India collided with the crust of Asia to form the Himalaya Mountains. Scientists believe these mountains are still pushing together and slowly rising.

The largest earthquake of the 20th century occurred in Chile on 22 May 1960. This quake registered 9.5 on the Richter Scale. The greatest number of people killed in one earthquake was in China in 1556. The quake killed about 830,000 people.

Tsunamis can be far-reaching and deadly. Waves from the 2004 Indian Ocean earthquake caused one of the deadliest disasters in recorded history. The tsunami killed nearly 300,000 people.

Tsunamis are caused by earthquakes, volcanic eruptions, or landslides. They can travel at speeds up to 966 kilometres (600 miles) per hour.

Researchers have discovered that rubber pads placed under earthquake-resistant buildings can cut the force of a quake by 25 percent.

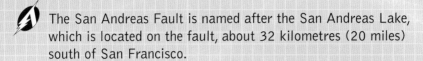 The San Andreas Fault is named after the San Andreas Lake, which is located on the fault, about 32 kilometres (20 miles) south of San Francisco.

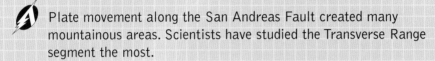 Plate movement along the San Andreas Fault created many mountainous areas. Scientists have studied the Transverse Range segment the most.

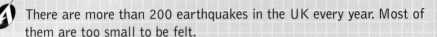 There are more than 200 earthquakes in the UK every year. Most of them are too small to be felt.

MORE ABOUT

Real name: Maxwell Axiom
Height: 1.86 m (6 ft 1 in.)
Weight: 87 kg (13 st. 10 lb.)
Eyes: Brown **Hair:** None

Super capabilities: Super intelligence; able to shrink to the size of an atom; sunglasses give X-ray vision; lab coat allows for travel through time and space.

Origin: Since birth, Max Axiom seemed destined for greatness. His mother, a marine biologist, taught her son about the mysteries of the sea. His father, a nuclear physicist and volunteer park warden, showed Max the wonders of the earth and sky.

One day, while Max was hiking in the hills, a megacharged lightning bolt struck him with blinding fury. When he awoke, he discovered a new-found energy and set out to learn as much about science as possible. He travelled the globe studying every aspect of the subject. Then he was ready to share his knowledge and new identity with the world. He had become Max Axiom, Super Scientist.

GLOSSARY

continental drift slow movement of the earth's continents

core inner part of the earth that is made of solid and molten metal

crust outer layer of the earth. The crust is thin and brittle compared to other layers of the earth.

detect notice or discover something

epicentre point on the earth's surface directly above the place where an earthquake occurs

fault crack in the earth's crust where two plates meet

fracture break or crack in something

magnitude measure of the amount of energy released by an earthquake

mantle layer of hot, dense rock that surrounds the earth's core

plate large sheet of rock that is a piece of the earth's crust

predict say what you think will happen in the future

rupture to break open or to burst

seismic caused by or related to an earthquake

seismogram written record of an earthquake

tsunami large, destructive wave caused by an underwater earthquake

volcanic eruption rock, hot ash, or lava thrown out of the earth with tremendous force

FIND OUT MORE

Books

The Asian Tsunami (When Disaster Struck series), John Townsend (Raintree, 2007)

How Does an Earthquake Become a Tsunami?, Linda Tagliaferro (Raintree, 2010)

How Does a Volcano Become an Island?, Linda Tagliaferro (Raintree, 2010)

Into the Fire: Volcanologists (Scientists at Work series), Paul Mason (Heinemann Library, 2007)

Websites

http://news.bbc.co.uk/cbbsnew
Enter "earthquakes' in the Search field to find out where earthquakes have been in the news, including how snakes can predict quakes!

http://www.nhm.ac.uk
Click on the "Kids only" tab of the Natural History Museum website, then click on "Earth and space" in the menu and go to the "Volcano" page to build a volcano online.

http://www.scholastic.com/magicschoolbus/games
Play "Blows Its Top" to get from the centre of the earth to the surface and find out some fun facts along the way.